FOR YOUR BIRTHDAY

FOR YOUR BIRTHDAY
By Snežana Pejaković-Kićović
Illustrated by Vladana Likar-Smiljanić
Translated by Zorka Mitrović
First published by Mladinska knjiga,
Ljubljana, Yugoslavia
Edited and adapted for the American
edition:
Pamela L. Espeland

ISBN 0 8317 3460-4
Printed and bound by Mladinska knjiga
Ljubljana, Yugoslavia

Snežana Pejaković-Kićović

€OR YOUR BIRTHDAY

Illustrated by Vladana Likar-Smiljanić

GALLERY BOOKS
An Imprint of W. H. Smith Publishers Inc.
112 Madison Avenue
New York City 10016

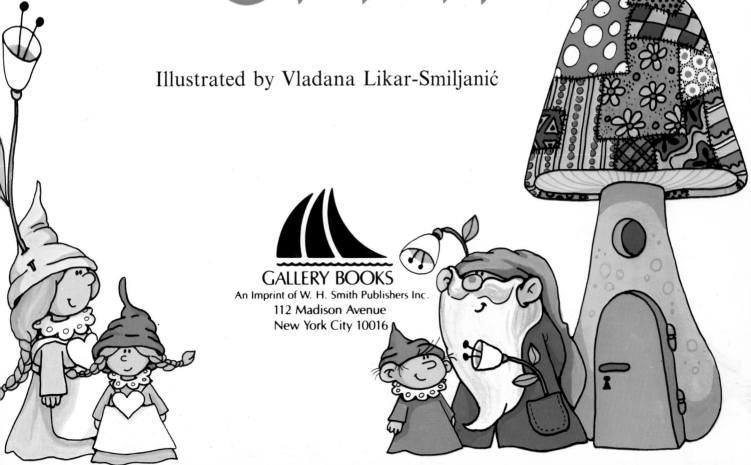

CONTENTS

FOR YOUR BIRTHDAY I will give you the sun. I will make it shine just for you. You will open your eyes in the morning, and there it will be. Warm and golden and shining just for you.

FOR YOUR BIRTHDAY I will give you the morning. Morning is when Mommy kisses you and says, »Wake up, my darling!« Morning is when the birds sing to welcome another day. Morning is when your Daddy pats your head and tells you to be good.

And while you are getting up and washing and dressing, I will give you another present FOR YOUR BIRTHDAY. A tiny spotted ladybug. Bright red, with bright white spots.

5

You know why ladybugs are special, don't you? Because they mean that company is coming soon. All sorts of strange, lovely, funny little guests.

Why are they coming? You know the answer.

FOR YOUR BIRTHDAY.

GUESTS
FROM
THE WOODS

Look who is here to wish you HAPPY BIRTHDAY! Over there, standing on that sawed-off tree limb. It's Mr. Cricket! Dressed up in his very best suit and getting ready to sing.

Be glad he CAN sing, for there was a time when he couldn't.

Long ago, Mr. Cricket's voice was much too rough and scratchy. Plus he didn't have an instrument to play. Still, he tried SO HARD to sing for his friends, the fairies and elves. They would join their hands to dance, and Mr. Cricket would climb up on his sawed-off tree limb and open his mouth wide. Then the most awful sounds would come out! SCRITCH SCRITCH, SQUEAK SQUEAK, SCRATCH SCRATCH, SCRITCH.

One day the King of the Fairies decided to help. He told the bees to bring the sweetest, smoothest honey from their hives and drip some into Mr. Cricket's throat. What a difference that made! Now Mr. Cricket's voice was sweet and smooth, just like the honey.

The Queen of the Fairies wanted to help, too. So she gave Mr. Cricket a violin and a bow. But first she sprinkled them both with dew and dried them in the moonlight. Now Mr. Cricket had an instrument to play!

If you sit VERY still, you will hear the song that Mr. Cricket wrote FOR YOUR BIRTHDAY. Listen for the sounds of his tiny violin.

I come from somewhere far away
To greet you on your special day.
The fairies wanted me to bring
A song that you can learn to sing.
The woodland elves, my special friends,
Send you a gift that never ends:
A bag of wishes just for you.
Try one now — it will come true!

When you have finished making your wish, please do something nice for Mr. Cricket. Clap your hands to thank him for his song.
Here is your next birthday guest. Say hello to Mrs. Snail!
There is something you should know about Mrs. Snail. She is one of the slowest creatures on earth. She is slower than a sunset. She is almost as slow as a stone.

On most days, everyone else has to wait for Mrs. Snail. But today is special. Mrs. Snail has arrived FOR YOUR BIRTHDAY — on time! Hurray for Mrs. Snail!

Mrs. Snail has brought you a present, too. It is a present you will treasure your whole life long. Before I tell you what it is, there is something else you should know about Mrs. Snail. Long ago, when Mrs. Snail first came into the world, she decided to carry her home with her everywhere. Now she never leaves it behind. Not when she goes for a walk. Not when she takes a bath in the rain. Not when she creeps into the garden to nibble on lettuce. Not even when Mr. Toad tries to nibble on her!

That is why she has brought it to your birthday. Look at her back and you will find it — Mrs. Snail's snug and cozy home.

Here is Mrs. Snail's present for you: Whenever you see her, you will think of YOUR home. Even when you are grown-up. Even if you move far away from your Mommy and Daddy. And you will feel snug and cozy, just like you feel today.

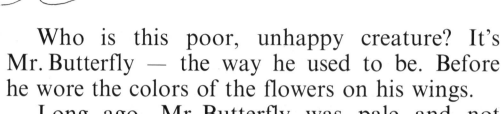

Who is this poor, unhappy creature? It's Mr. Butterfly — the way he used to be. Before he wore the colors of the flowers on his wings.

Long ago, Mr. Butterfly was pale and not at all pretty. He wanted to be friends with the elves and the fairies, but none of them would play with him. This made Mr. Butterfly so sad that he flew from flower to flower, crying. He left a teardrop on every one.

The flowers felt sorry for Mr. Butterfly and decided to help him. Whenever they caught one of

16

his tears, they mixed it with the colors from their petals. Then they painted his wings!

The forget-me-not brought blue. The daisy added white. The bluebell offered purple. The dandelion gave yellow. Finally the poppy streaked Mr. Butterfly's wings with red.

Mr. Butterfly fluttered with joy.
He was beautiful!

18

Now the elves opened the gates to their homes and let Mr. Butterfly inside. And each night the fairies set a place for him at their table.

What has Mr. Butterfly brought FOR YOUR BIRTH-DAY? The blue of the sky. The white of the snow. Sunshine yellow and the pink of your cheeks. The purple of a soft night shadow. All the brilliant colors of his powdery wings.

Who's next? It's Miss Centipede! You probably already know that Miss Centipede is famous all over the world. She is good at sports, and she is very kind. This is her story. Are you listening?

Long ago the King of the Fairies invited many guests to dinner. They had too much to eat and drink and stayed much too long at the table. Most of them had even fallen asleep at their plates! How rude!

The King of the Fairies yawned loudly and stood up. Then he shook his cloak and stomped toward the door. He was angry because his guests had such bad manners.

Miss Centipede, who was sitting at the end of the table, was still awake. She noticed the King's anger. So she jumped up and ran after him on her many, many feet.

"Your Majesty!" she cried. "Please wait!"

"What do YOU want?" the King asked in a grumpy voice.

Miss Centipede kneeled before him on her many, many knees. Then she looked up at him. "Your feast has been so wonderful that it should end with something wonderful."

"What do you mean?" the King wanted to know.

"Let's have a race!" Miss Centipede said. "The fastest among your guests can compete, and everyone else can bet on who will win!"

"That's great idea!" the King shouted. Then he told one of his servants to wake everyone up and announce the news.

"Attention! Attention! A race! A race!" shouted the servant. "You will all run to the prickly plant on top of the hill. The first one to pick a flower and bring it back, wins!"

The guests all rubbed their eyes and started talking at once.

Now the Queen of the Fairies was sure that Mr. Dragonfly would win. She bet her own pearl necklace on it. Then Mr. Bumblebee threw a purse full of gold coins on the table and buzzed, "I bet on Mr. Worm!"

Many of the guests were surprised by Bumblebee's choice. Poky old Mr. Worm? How could he win a race against Mr. Dragonfly? But Mr. Bumblebee thought to himself, "They don't know that a storm is coming. Those who fly will get their wings soaked. Those who crawl will slide down the hill. But Mr. Worm will burrow underground and easily reach the top!"

Nobody bet on Miss Centipede, and that made her sad. Then, all at once, a wise old dwarf spoke up.

"I have no pearls or gold coins," he said, "but I think that Miss Centipede will win."

"And what will you bet?" asked the king. The dwarf spread his hands and shrugged.

"I know!" said Mr. Bumblebee. "Let him bet his beard! Then we can shave it off when he loses!"

His beard was all he had, so the wise old dwarf agreed.

The referee blew his whistle. The race was on! Everyone flew, and crawled, and slithered, and burrowed their way toward the hill. Suddenly it began to rain. Then it began to pour. Water fell from the sky in sheets!

Mr. Dragonfly tumbled to the ground with soggy wings. And Mr. Worm, who was digging his way underground, ran into an enormous rock. It was so big he could not get around it.

Meanwhile Miss Centipede hurried along on her many, many legs. She did not think about the heavy rain. She did not think about the mud. She did not think about being cold and wet and uncomfortable. She thought only about the poor but govd and very wise old dwarf, and how he deeply believed in her, and how he would feel if he lost his beard.

She reached the prickly plant, picked a flower, and slid back down the hill. Miss Centipede had won!

The Queen of the Fairies was furious. So was Mr. Bumblebee. But they had to hand over their bets anyway. They gave the pearls and the gold coins to the King, who gave them in turn to Miss Centipede and the dwarf.

All the dwarf really wanted was his beard, though. And all Miss Centipede wanted was for the dwarf to be happy. So they didn't keep the pearls and the coins.

Nobody is quite sure what happened to them.
Maybe YOU will find them someday.

One more guest is arriving FOR YOUR BIRTHDAY. When you see him, don't be afraid. It's MR. SPIDER!

He may be ugly, and he may not seem very friendly at first, but I think you will like him anyway. For he is bringing a present, too.

You probably think that spiders only spin webs. Not our friend Mr. Spider! He also spins stories. Very special stories.

Would you like to hear them now?

26

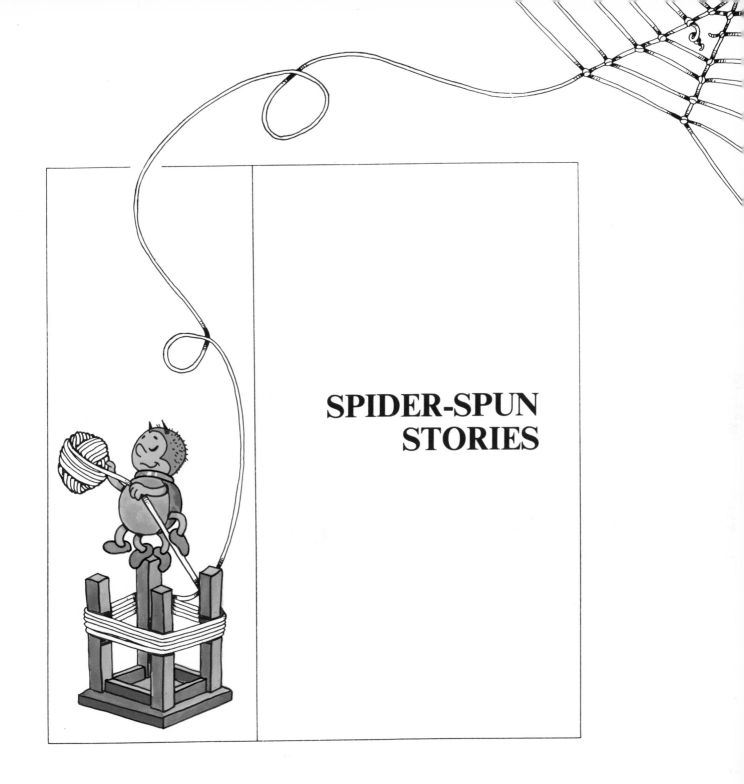

SPIDER-SPUN
STORIES

Mr. Spider's First Story: Spring

"We are back!" the storks cried, flapping their big wings and sailing down to the edge of the chimney.

"They are back!" croaked the frog, diving into the pool as fast as he could. (Did you know that storks EAT frogs? Well, they do!)

"They are back!" whispered the flowers. The primroses, daisies, and violets raised their heads to see.

"They are back!" mumbled the finch. She had a bit of straw in her beak and had to talk around it. The straw, of course, was for her brand-new nest.

"They are back!" hummed the breeze, touching the egg in the bluebird's nest. All at once, the eggshell cracked, and out popped a tiny blue head!

"My baby is born!" cried the bluebird at the top of her voice. "My beautiful little baby is born!"

"We are back," sang all the birds together. "We have brought the spring, the birthday of the world!"

Mr. Spider's Second Story: Summer

"I am the brightest," bragged the apple.

"I am the juiciest," boasted the peach.

"I am the tastiest," crowed the apricot.

"I am the ripest," claimed the pear, swinging fatly from a branch.

"Nobody is sweeter than we are," said the grapes. They puffed up so far their purple skins nearly burst.

"But the dwarves like me best of all," announced the plum. "They pick me even when I am not ripe!"

Just then some dwarves came along, carrying a basket. They picked an apple, a peach, an apricot, a pear, a bunch of grapes, and a plum. They put them into the basket and started toward home.

"What beautiful fruit!" said one of the dwarves.

"And how lucky we are, to find all of our favorites!" said another.

Who knows if the apple is the brightest, or the peach is the juiciest, or the apricot is the tastiest, or the pear is the ripest, or the grapes are the sweetest, or the plum is the best of all? When EVERY bite of fruit tastes good, who cares?

Mr. Spider's Third Story: Autumn

"It is autumn," said the elves. "Time to squeeze the grapes into wine."

"It is autumn," said the
dwarves. "Time to husk the
corn and store it in our barns."

"It is autumn," whistled the wind.
"Time to blow the leaves off the trees."

The leaves started dancing in the air.
Red, yellow, brown and green, they
whirled and twirled in the wind.

The bees danced, too. When they grew tired of dancing, they flew back to their tree-trunk home and shut the door against the wind. The leaves danced on and on.

Suddenly a heavy rain fell from the sky. It fell into the brook and filled it up, all the way to its banks. The brook had never been so big and powerful! "Look at me!" it growled. "See how big and powerful I am!"

Next, frost covered the grass until every blade wore a crystal coat.

"It is going to be a long winter," sighed the squirrels. "Time to gather acorns so we will have enough to eat."

"It is going to be a long winter," agreed the ants. "Autumn is coming to an end. We must hurry, hurry, hurry!"

Only the hedgehog was ready. She was sound asleep under her patchwork quilt. There was plenty of wood for her stove, and her slippers were tucked neatly beneath her bed.

Sweet dreams, little hedgehog!

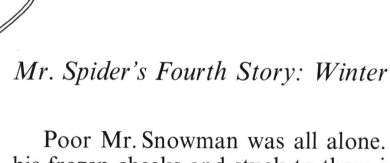

Mr. Spider's Fourth Story: Winter

Poor Mr. Snowman was all alone. Tears ran down his frozen cheeks and stuck to them in ugly lumps.

"Where are my friends?" he wondered. "How sad and dull it is without them!"

Then, from high in the air, came a chorus of tiny voices, saying, "Here we are! Here we are! Don't be lonely, don't be sad!"

Snowflakes were tumbling from all directions. Mr. Snowman's friends had come at last!

"Look! It's snowing!" cried the sparrow, balancing on a branch.

The gray rabbit hopped over to Mr. Snowman and raised a furry paw. He brushed some of the frozen tears away from Mr. Snowman's cheeks.

The brown squirrel skipped over to Mr. Snowman and raised his bushy tail. He wiped more of the frozen tears away.

The spotted fawn tiptoed over to Mr. Snowman and stuck out his warm, pink tongue. She licked some of the frozen tears and melted the rest with her breath.

Mr. Snowman smiled. How handsome he looked, with his cheeks all smooth and shiny again!

I hope YOU are smiling, too!

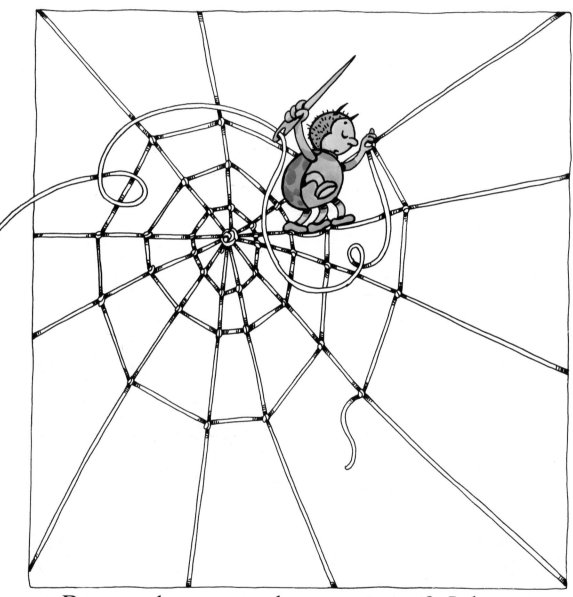

Do you have enough presents yet? I hope not, because I have more **FOR YOUR BIRTHDAY**. Many, many more! Including some that SEEM very ordinary. See what you think!

SOME VERY ORDINARY THINGS

Every child likes the seaside, for visiting or for living by. Here are some very ordinary things for you to use when you are there.

A Little Rubber Raft. Row it with the oars, or row it with your hands. It doesn't matter. But go quickly to the nearest island. There you will find a curious lizard who has wandered there by mistake. Pick him up, put him into your raft, and take him back to shore. His worried mother is waiting for him!

A Diving Mask. Pull it on over your eyes, take a DEEP breath, and dive down into the blue water. Stay in the shallow part and look for a sleepy sea-urchin. Next to him is an empty seashell that nobody has lived in for a very long time. Take it home and keep it for your granny.

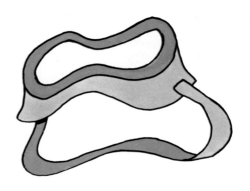

Grannies like the sea, but they should not stay in the hot sun for long. Give your granny the seashell and tell her this: "The next time you wish you could go to the seaside, hold the shell up to your ear. You will hear the whistling wind and the roaring waves."

For the seashell is not REALLY empty. Inside it is the song of the sea. It will make your granny happy and soothe her to sleep.

A small white sailboat. Leave it where it is! Soon a frightened bee will land on it. Children playing on the beach will splash her wings, and she will need a safe place to dry them.

A lantern made of metal and glass. Light it one night before the moon rises. Then hold it over a corner of the dark, dark sea. A little lost fish will be down there. Use your lantern to guide her safely home.

Every child likes the mountains, too. Have you ever been there? Would you like to go? Here are some very ordinary things to take along.

Little green hats with flowers and feathers. How many would you like? Be sure to take enough for all your friends. The flowers come from mountains called the Alps. People who wear them on their hats look like real mountain climbers.

A pair of magic boots. These will take you to the top of any mountain in a single step! If you don't believe this, put them on the paws of the old sheepdog who has spent his life guarding sheep in the high pastures. He is getting tired of climbing, and he will be grateful to you.

A tiny spotted umbrella. Real mountain climbers never use an umbrella, so you will probably want to give this away. Halfway up the mountain you will find a nest of baby birds. The umbrella is for them, to protect their fuzzy heads the next time it storms.

Every child LOVES the country. There is so much room to play! Here are some very ordinary things that are just right for the country.

A hoe and a spade. Use these to break up the land and dig some holes. Throw seeds into the holes. Add water. Wait for something nice to grow.

A rooster with a rainbow tail. When you are in the country, you will want to get up early. But you will not need an alarm clock. This rooster will wake you at the crack of dawn with his COCK-A-DOODLE--DOO.

A saltshaker full of salt. Pour some into the palm of your hand. Then hold out your hand to the calf with the pink nose. The calf will lick your hand, and it will tickle!

A curry-comb. That old horse in the barn needs a good grooming. Ever since the farmer bought a tractor, the horse has had nothing to do. He used to pull the plough and the hay-wagon, but now he spends his days all alone and bored. Brush him properly until he shines. Then ride him in the next parade. How proud he will be!

Do you have enough ordinary things? Good, because I have run out of them.

Now it's time for some UNUSUAL things. Peculiar things. Weird things. Things you can only find in three strange stories.

THREE
STRANGE
STORIES

The Giant Appledapple

Once upon a time there was a whole village that floated in the air. Houses and cottages hung there, day after day, like clouds. And right in the middle of them floated a giant's castle.

The name of the giant was Mr. Appledapple. He was a very greedy giant. He ate anything he found. He didn't care if it was a roasted chicken, a pan of cornbread, or a piece of firewood. Into his mouth it went. CHOMP CHOMP!

And when he ran out of things to eat, he gobbled up his neighbors'.

Luckily someone discovered Mr. Appledapple's favorite food. Big, sweet, juicy, ripe-red apples. And luckily someone else discovered an apple tree. It was growing in the ground right under the giant's castle.

Mr. Appledapple's servants and neighbors started watering the tree. They watered it so much that it bore huge, shiny apples all year round.

When Mr. Appledapple noticed the apple tree, he simply **HAD** to taste its fruit.

He lowered a thick rope and climbed down to the earth.

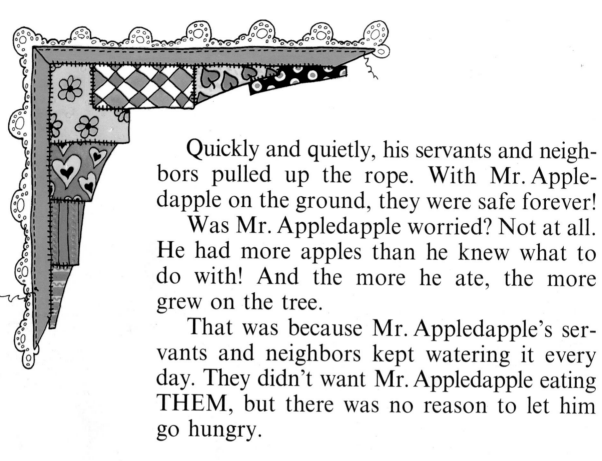

Quickly and quietly, his servants and neighbors pulled up the rope. With Mr. Appledapple on the ground, they were safe forever!

Was Mr. Appledapple worried? Not at all. He had more apples than he knew what to do with! And the more he ate, the more grew on the tree.

That was because Mr. Appledapple's servants and neighbors kept watering it every day. They didn't want Mr. Appledapple eating THEM, but there was no reason to let him go hungry.

They were really very kind-hearted
after all.

The Plant-Eating Dragon

Speaking of giants, there was another kind that lived a VERY long time ago. Millions of millions of years ago. Before there were even any people in the world.

Most giants you read about are mean and greedy, right? And most dragons you read about are just plain nasty. They come up out of lakes or run out of caves and spit fire or bite brave knights.

The very first nasty dragon probably wasn't a dragon after all. It was probably a dinosaur called Tyrannosaurus Rex. Maybe you have seen pictures of him. As big as a building! Covered with scales! A mouth full of terrible teeth!

But what about gentle dragons? There must have been some of them, too! And, in fact, there were. But they weren't really dragons, either. They were dinosaurs, just like T. Rex.

One was named Brontosaurus. He was as long as a pirate ship. He weighed as much as a dozen elephants. But he didn't use his size to frighten other creatures. And he only ate plants.

Here is a picture of Brontosaurus for you to look at. (Uhoh! Someone else is in the picture, too. Do you know who it is?)

The Little Witch

Once there was a little witch who wanted to be a Real Witch. But first she had to pass a test at the Witches' School. To help prepare for her test, she bought a cauldron for mixing potions. Then she hired four assistants — a raven, two mice, and a red-bearded dwarf.

But the dwarf secretly HATED witches. He set about trying to spoil her spells so she would flunk her test!

One day the little witch sent the raven on an errand. "Go to the Wormwood Valley," she said, "and bring back some Prickly-stickly." When the raven returned with the Prickly-stickly, the dwarf stole it and hid it. Then he threw some Stickly-prickly into the cauldron instead.

The next day the little witch sent the two mice on an errand. "Go to the Wormwood Forest," she said, "and bring back some Itchy-scritchy." When the mice returned with the Itchy-scritchy, the dwarf stole it and hid it. Then he threw some Scritchy-itchy into the cauldron instead.

The next day the little witch caught a frog and brought it home. Then she told it to jump into the cauldron and swim — just for a minute. "You can jump right out again," she told the frog, "but QUIET while you're in there. No croaking!" When the frog was in the cauldron, the dwarf

sneaked up and scared him. The frog couldn't help it —
he croaked!

Finally the little witch was ready to stir the potion.
Now remember that she was just learning how to be
a Real Witch, so there were still many things she didn't
know. For example, you NEVER stir a cauldron
clockwise. You ALWAYS stir it COUNTER-clockwise.

The dwarf knew this, of course. But he didn't tell
the little witch. Instead, he watched her stir the cauldron
clockwise!

Finally the potion was ready. It LOOKED like it
should. It SMELLED like it should. So the little
witch put out the fire, let the potion cool, poured

some into a jug, and took three big swallows. Then she poured the rest into a special bottle and put it in her pocket. She was ready for her test. She would be a Real Witch at last!

She went before the Witches' Council. "You must perform four tasks," the Head Witch said. "First, kill the lilac tree in the village garden. Then steal five hens from a henhouse — without making any noise! Then cast a spell on a freshwater spring and dry it up. Finally, fly your broom over the village and cackle as loudly as you can."

The tasks all sounded so easy! The little witch KNEW she could do them, one after another.

First the little witch sprinkled the lilac tree with her magic potion. But instead of turning brown and dying, the lilac burst into blossom! It filled the whole village with its sweet perfume.

The little witch hurried on to the henhouse. She said a Silence Spell over herself and prepared to steal five hens. But instead of moving quietly, she made a terrible racket! Of course the watchdog awoke. The little witch got away — but not before the watchdog took a bite out of her skirt!

Next she found the freshwater spring. She dripped a few drops of her potion into it. But instead of drying up, the spring swelled and flowed even more quickly! Water gushed out in gallons and streamed downhill.

The little witch knew that she had ONE MORE CHANCE. She climbed onto her broom, practiced her cackle, and flew into the air. For luck, she sipped from her bottle.

But instead of cackling, the most beautiful song came out of her throat! It sounded like birds singing at sunrise.

By now everyone in the village was wide awake. They smelled the lilacs, they heard the freshwater spring gurgling, and they heard the little witch's beautiful song. They got out of bed and walked outside to look around.

The little witch was frightened and VERY worried. What if somebody saw her? She sprinkled the rest of her magic potion over her broom. "Take me away from this place, and HURRY," she commanded. Instead, the end of her broom turned into a bouquet of flowers! It whirled the little witch through the air and landed on top of a tall oak tree.

59

The little witch scurried down the trunk and ran straight into the tiny house you see here. (Lucky for her, nobody lived in it.) She slammed the door behind her, and there she stayed. She is inside right now. If you knock on the door, she probably won't come out.

SOMETHING
YOU AREN'T
EXPECTING

I know that you will not mind if I give you an animal FOR YOUR BIRTHDAY. What about a cat or a dog? An old tortoise, a white mouse, or a colorful parrot? No, I think I will give you something else instead. A small gray donkey!

Why would I give you a donkey? Because hardly anyone has a donkey these days. Have you ever even seen one up close? I didn't think so.

Here is your donkey now. Poor thing — just look at him! There he stands under the hot noonday sun, loaded down with heavy packs. He sighs. He sighs again. He is SO unhappy. Later, when he gets home and somebody takes those packs off of him, he will start to bray and cry. Why? Because most children have forgotten all about him!

Let's do something about that right now. Tell your parents that you want a REAL donkey for your birthday. Tell them that he can stay in your room and you will take care of him. Tell them that you will feed him and brush his coat and let him sleep in your bed. Then tell your friends to ask their parents for donkeys, too.

Everybody should have a donkey, don't you think?

Can you imagine what is inside these bags? More presents! I hope you are good at counting. Because these bags are full of numbers FOR YOUR BIRHDAY.

SOME
NUMBERS
FOR YOU

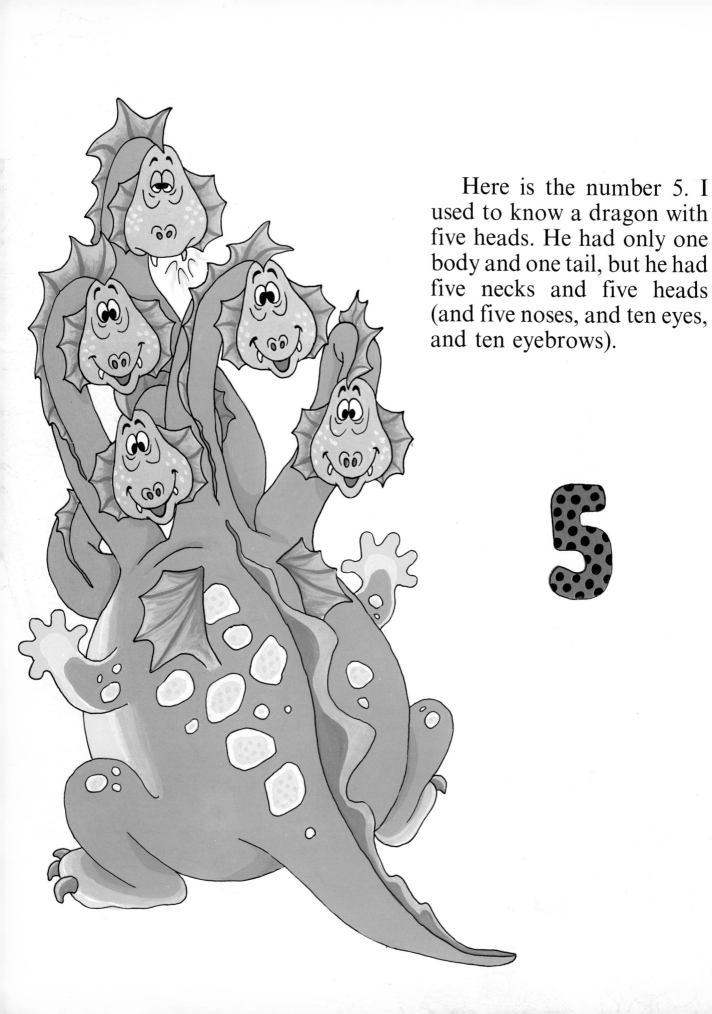

Here is the number 5. I used to know a dragon with five heads. He had only one body and one tail, but he had five necks and five heads (and five noses, and ten eyes, and ten eyebrows).

5

If you have a five-layered birthday cake, you had better cut five big pieces in a hurry. Because the dragon I used to know is coming to your house, and he is VERY hungry. His favorite food in the whole world is five-layered birthday cake. Unless you can find five knights with five swords, you had better give him what he wants.

If you DO find five knights, maybe you should share your birthday cake with them.

Here is the number 4. Maybe that is a better number to give you, since there are no four--headed dragons.

There ARE four-leaf clovers, though. You probably know that four-leaf clovers bring luck. If you ever find one, pick it carefully and press it between the pages of a heavy book. Then save it for the rest of your life.

The first leaf will bring luck to you. The second leaf will bring luck to your whole family — your Mommy, your Daddy, any brothers or sisters you have, your old granny, your grandpa, and all of your aunts and uncles and cousins. The third leaf will bring luck to your best friend. And the fourth leaf will bring luck to anyone you choose.

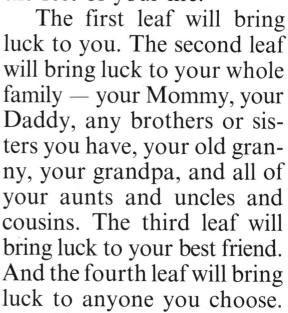

Here is the number 2. And here are two camels, each with two humps. Two little Bedouins are sitting on the camels, and each Bedouin has hung two bags from each side of his camel.

How many bags are there in all? Did you count eight? Good, because there is something for you inside each bag.

In the first bag you will find a loaf of bread. Take it to the park, crumble it, and feed the pigeons. They will be very glad to see you.

In the second bag you will find a little stone. It belongs to a naughty boy named Larry, who likes to throw it at birds. Take the stone and put it in your pocket. The next time you are passing by a river or a stream, toss the stone into the water so Larry can never find it again.

In the third bag you will find a watering can. Please fill it and water that pretty blue flower — the one that is drooping because it is so thirsty.

In the fourth bag you will find a flute. Take it out and look at it VERY closely. Does it seem like an ordinary flute? A fierce snake once thought so, too.

One morning a little Indian boy caught the snake and put it into a covered basket. At first the little boy didn't know what to do with the snake. Every other living creature he had ever met wanted to be friendly with him, but the snake just hissed and showed its fangs and stuck out its tongue.

The little Indian boy thought and thought. Finally he had an idea. He carved a flute from a willow branch. Then he played it for the snake. It was the sweetest, most beautiful sound the snake had ever heard.

The snake forgot all about biting the little boy and started dancing to the music. No wonder. Music works magic everywhere in the world. Old and young, people and animals, even plants love music. What about YOU?

In the fifth bag you will find a thin and dangerous- -looking stick. Why would I give you a stick? Here is the reason: I have heard that sticks like this one still hang on the wall in some houses. And I have heard that some mommies and daddies, when they get VERY angry, use them to punish their naughty children.

But if a little Indian boy could charm a fierce snake with music, then a kind word should be enough to help a naughty child behave. So I would like you to take this stick, break it in two, and throw it far away.

In the sixth bag you will find a big, tasty bone. Any dog in the world would love to have this bone.

Did you know that some dogs don't belong to anybody? That nobody takes care of them or feeds them?

Maybe someday you will meet a dog like this. Save the bone until then and give it to the dog. He will be so grateful that perhaps he will lick your hand.

In the seventh bag you will find a genuine double-
-barreled shotgun. I know that YOU will never use
it to shoot any living creature, so that is why I am
giving it to you. Hide it away carefully so a hunter
can never find it. Then imagine how happy the rabbits,
pheasants, and deer will be!

In the eighth bag you will find a bar of chocolate. All of us feel like eating chocolate at the wrong times — just when Mommy is getting dinner ready, or when she is calling us to the table. How good it would be to take a single bite of chocolate at that very moment!

That is why I thought you should have a whole bar of your own. Store it in a safe place and nibble on it whenever you're not supposed to. I won't tell if YOU won't.

The last number I want to give you is the number 1.

Why did I leave it for the end, when we all know that it usually comes at the beginning? Because I wanted to remind you that there is only one Mommy, only one Daddy, only one sun, one heart, and one home.

And of course, there is only one YOU.

Here are some leftover numbers. Maybe we will get around to them next year.

**HAPPY
BIRTHDAY
FROM
EVERYONE
EVERYWHERE**

If you put all of the numbers I gave you into a line, here is what you will get:

5 4 2 8 1

It looks like part of a telephone number. Try dialing it (plus a few more numbers) and if you are lucky somebody's telephone may ring somewhere in the world... and the person who answers may wish you Happy Birthday in his or her own language.

RING! A little Iraqui girl answers and says,

Iid milad seaid!

RING! A Mongolian boy answers and says,
Toursoun oudrin chin bayar hurgeye!

RING! A young Russian girl answers and say,
Stchastlyivy dyen rozhdeniya!

RING! A girl from the Congo
answers and says,
Fuwha mraka mpya!

RING! A little American Indian
boy greets you in his language…
RING! And so does an Eskimo.
(Listen closely, and you may hear the
sounds of whistling winds and
drifting snows.)

RING? Please be patient. This Japanese girl is waiting for her mommy to answer the telephone.

ALMOST
THE END

You are almost at the end of this book. And maybe you are almost at the end of your birthday.

Is the sun going down? Have you put on your pajamas and brushed your teeth? Then it must be bedtime.

Look outside your window. Can you see the moon shining in the sky? (If it is not there, it will be in a day or so. Or perhaps it is hiding behind a cloud.)

I give you the moon FOR YOUR BIRTHDAY. All night long, it will shine its silvery light into your room. You don't have to be afraid of the dark because the moon will be there, shining just for you.

And when you fall asleep I will give you one last present: love. Love is what made my child grow up to be big and happy. Love is what makes *all* children grow up to be big and happy. I know it will for you, too.

Lay your head on your pillow. Tuck your blanket under your chin. Now close your eyes and think about your birthday.

Not THIS one, but the one you will have NEXT year!